THE MARVELOUS LAND OF OZ

VOL. 4

ADAPTED FROM THE NOVEL BY L. FRANK BAUM

Writer: **ERIC SHANOWER**
Artist: **SKOTTIE YOUNG**
Colorist: **JEAN-FRANCOIS BEAULIEU**
Letterer: **JEFF ECKLEBERRY**

Assistant Editor: **MICHAEL HORWITZ**
Editor: **NATE COSBY**

Collection Editor: **MARK D. BEAZLEY**
Assistant Editors: **ALEX STARBUCK & NELSON RIBEIRO**
Editor, Special Projects: **JENNIFER GRÜNWALD**
Senior Editor, Special Projects: **JEFF YOUNGQUIST**
SVP of Print & Digital Publishing Sales: **DAVID GABRIEL**
Production: **JERRY KALINOWSKI**
Book Design: **ARLENE SO**

Editor in Chief: **AXEL ALONSO**
Chief Creative Officer: **JOE QUESADA**
Publisher: **DAN BUCKLEY**
Executive Producer: **ALAN FINE**

Spotlight

MARVEL

visit us at www.abdopublishing.com

Reinforced library bound edition published in 2014 by Spotlight, a division of the ABDO Group, PO Box 398166, Minneapolis, Minnesota 55439. Spotlight produces high-quality reinforced library bound editions for schools and libraries. Published by agreement with Marvel Characters, Inc.

Printed in the United States of America, North Mankato, Minnesota.
102013
012014
This book contains at least 10% recycled materials.

Marvel.com
© 2014 Marvel

Library of Congress Cataloging-in-Publication Data

Shanower, Eric.
  The marvelous land of Oz / adapted from the novel by L. Frank Baum ; writer: Eric Shanower ; artist: Skottie Young. -- Reinforced library bound edition.
     pages cm
  "Marvel."
  Summary: When the Scarecrow, now the ruler of the Emerald City, is driven out by General Jinjur and her all-girl army, his friends--the Tin Woodman, a boy named Tip, and Jack Pumpkinhead--try to restore peace in this graphic novel adaptation of L. Frank Baum's classic tale.
  ISBN 978-1-61479-235-2 (vol. 1) -- ISBN 978-1-61479-236-9 (vol. 2) -- ISBN 978-1-61479-237-6 (vol. 3) -- ISBN 978-1-61479-238-3 (vol. 4) -- ISBN 978-1-61479-239-0 (vol. 5) -- ISBN 978-1-61479-240-6 (vol. 6) -- ISBN 978-1-61479-241-3 (vol. 7) -- ISBN 978-1-61479-242-0 (vol. 8)
  1. Graphic novels. [1. Graphic novels. 2. Fantasy.] I. Young, Skottie, illustrator. II. Baum, L. Frank (Lyman Frank), 1856-1919. Marvelous land of Oz. III. Title.
  PZ7.7.S453Mar 2014
  741.5'973--dc23
                              2013030127

All Spotlight books are reinforced library binding and manufactured in the United States of America.

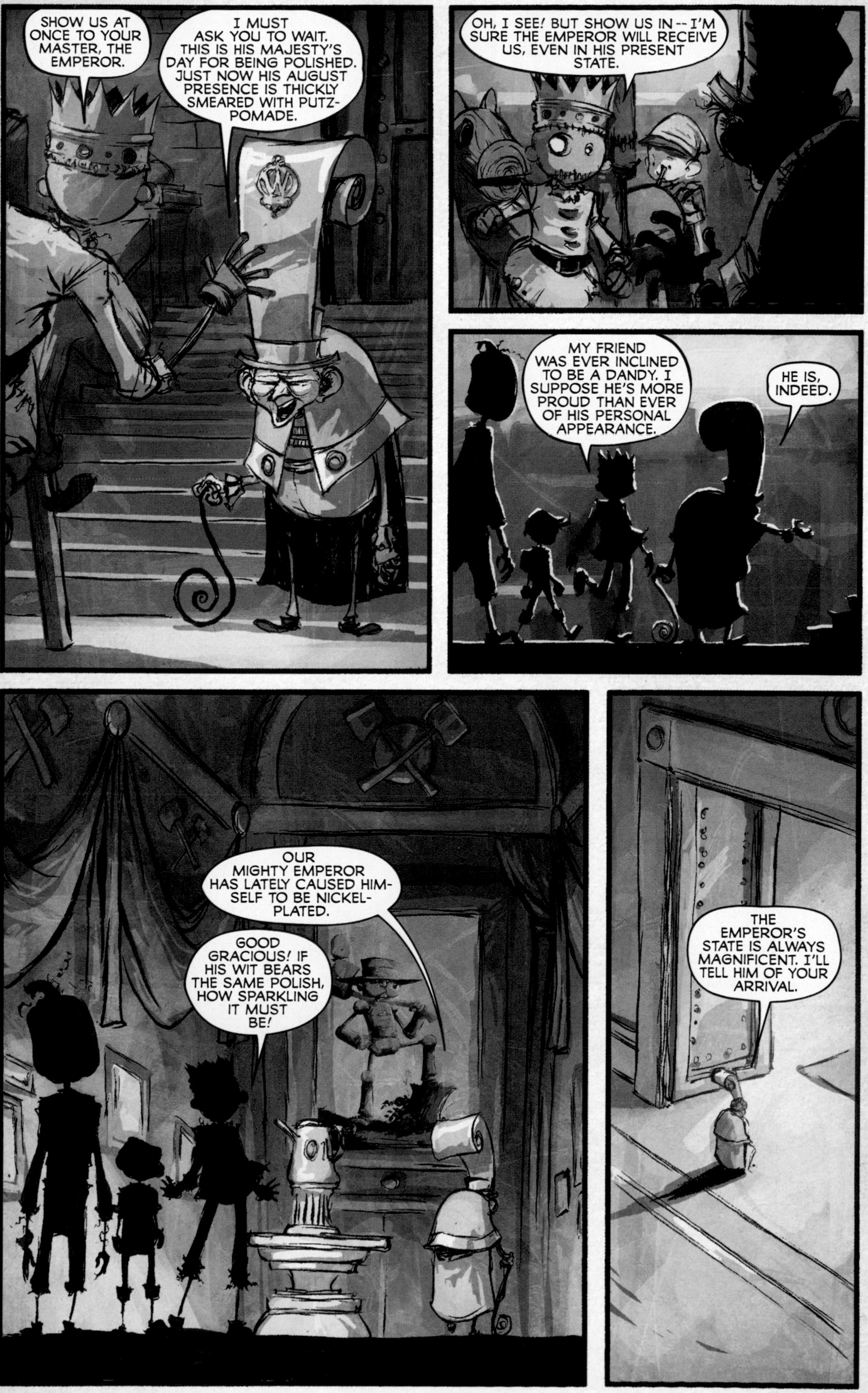
SHOW US AT ONCE TO YOUR MASTER, THE EMPEROR.
I MUST ASK YOU TO WAIT. THIS IS HIS MAJESTY'S DAY FOR BEING POLISHED. JUST NOW HIS AUGUST PRESENCE IS THICKLY SMEARED WITH PUTZ-POMADE.
OH, I SEE! BUT SHOW US IN -- I'M SURE THE EMPEROR WILL RECEIVE US, EVEN IN HIS PRESENT STATE.
MY FRIEND WAS EVER INCLINED TO BE A DANDY. I SUPPOSE HE'S MORE PROUD THAN EVER OF HIS PERSONAL APPEARANCE.
HE IS, INDEED.
OUR MIGHTY EMPEROR HAS LATELY CAUSED HIM-SELF TO BE NICKEL-PLATED.
GOOD GRACIOUS! IF HIS WIT BEARS THE SAME POLISH, HOW SPARKLING IT MUST BE!
THE EMPEROR'S STATE IS ALWAYS MAGNIFICENT. I'LL TELL HIM OF YOUR ARRIVAL.

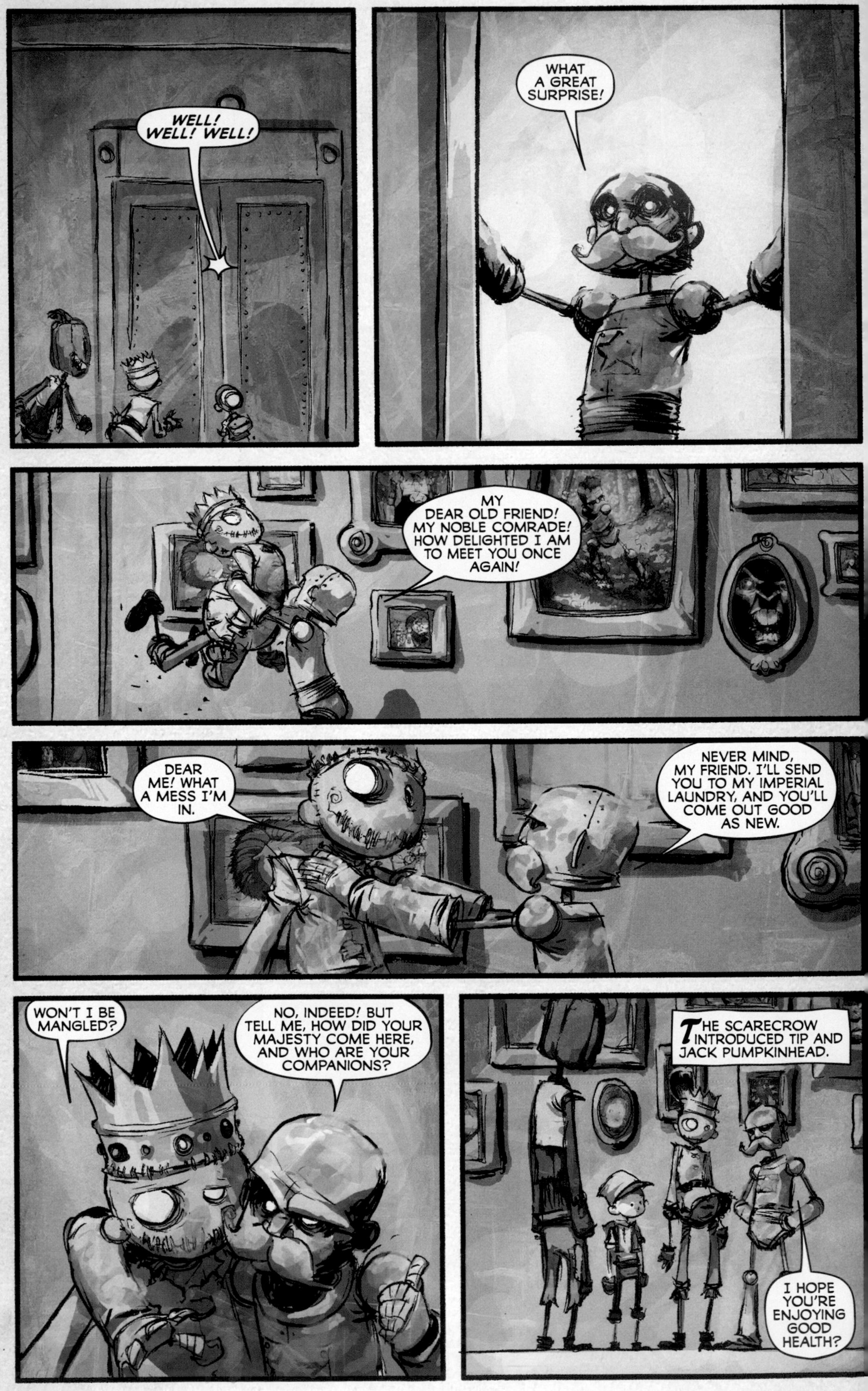
WELL! WELL! WELL!
WHAT A GREAT SURPRISE!
MY DEAR OLD FRIEND! MY NOBLE COMRADE! HOW DELIGHTED I AM TO MEET YOU ONCE AGAIN!
DEAR ME! WHAT A MESS I'M IN.
NEVER MIND, MY FRIEND. I'LL SEND YOU TO MY IMPERIAL LAUNDRY, AND YOU'LL COME OUT GOOD AS NEW.
WON'T I BE MANGLED?
NO, INDEED! BUT TELL ME, HOW DID YOUR MAJESTY COME HERE, AND WHO ARE YOUR COMPANIONS?
THE SCARECROW INTRODUCED TIP AND JACK PUMPKINHEAD.
I HOPE YOU'RE ENJOYING GOOD HEALTH?

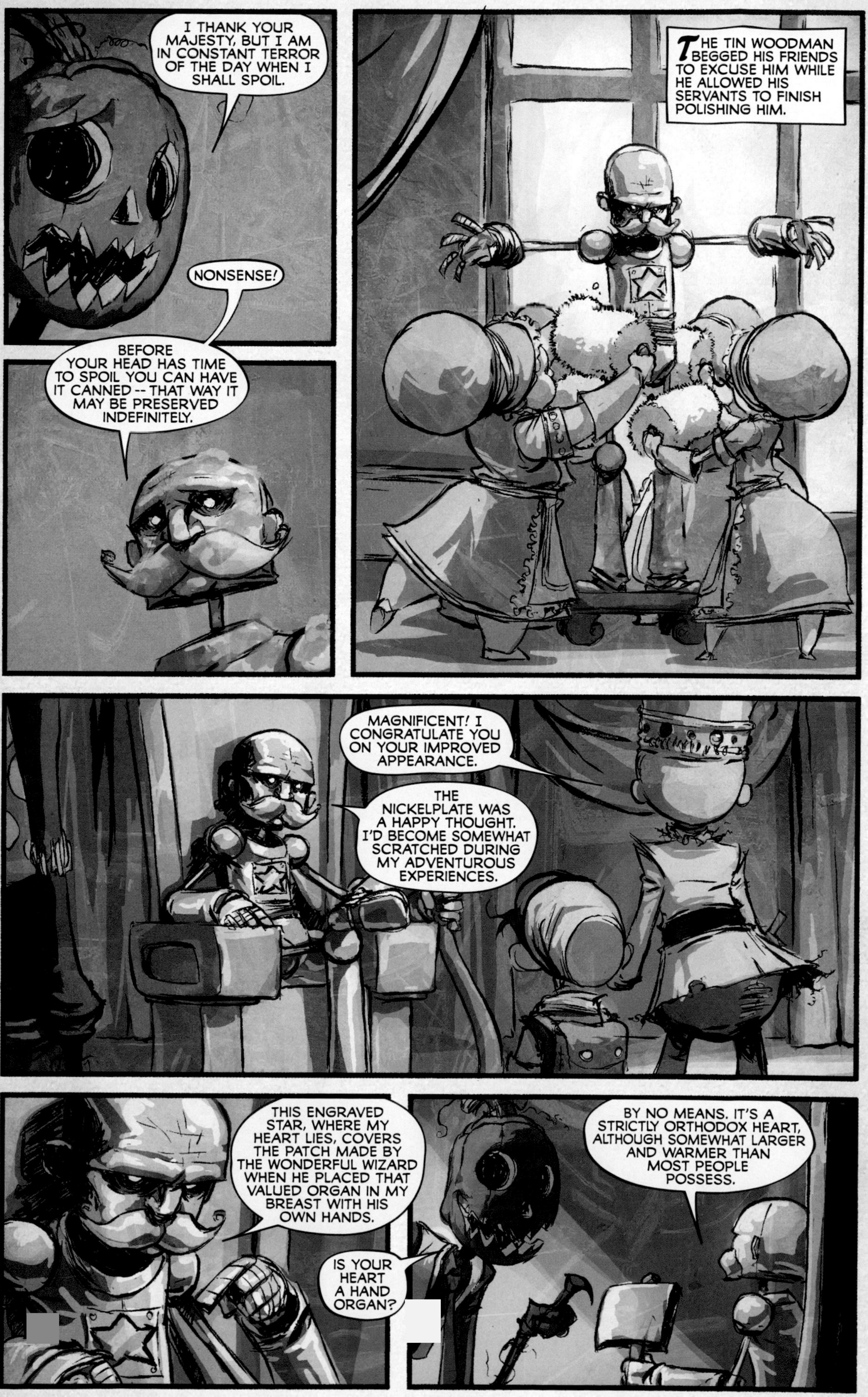
I THANK YOUR MAJESTY, BUT I AM IN CONSTANT TERROR OF THE DAY WHEN I SHALL SPOIL.
NONSENSE!
BEFORE YOUR HEAD HAS TIME TO SPOIL YOU CAN HAVE IT CANNED -- THAT WAY IT MAY BE PRESERVED INDEFINITELY.
THE TIN WOODMAN BEGGED HIS FRIENDS TO EXCUSE HIM WHILE HE ALLOWED HIS SERVANTS TO FINISH POLISHING HIM.
MAGNIFICENT! I CONGRATULATE YOU ON YOUR IMPROVED APPEARANCE.
THE NICKELPLATE WAS A HAPPY THOUGHT. I'D BECOME SOMEWHAT SCRATCHED DURING MY ADVENTUROUS EXPERIENCES.
THIS ENGRAVED STAR, WHERE MY HEART LIES, COVERS THE PATCH MADE BY THE WONDERFUL WIZARD WHEN HE PLACED THAT VALUED ORGAN IN MY BREAST WITH HIS OWN HANDS.
IS YOUR HEART A HAND ORGAN?
BY NO MEANS. IT'S A STRICTLY ORTHODOX HEART, ALTHOUGH SOMEWHAT LARGER AND WARMER THAN MOST PEOPLE POSSESS.

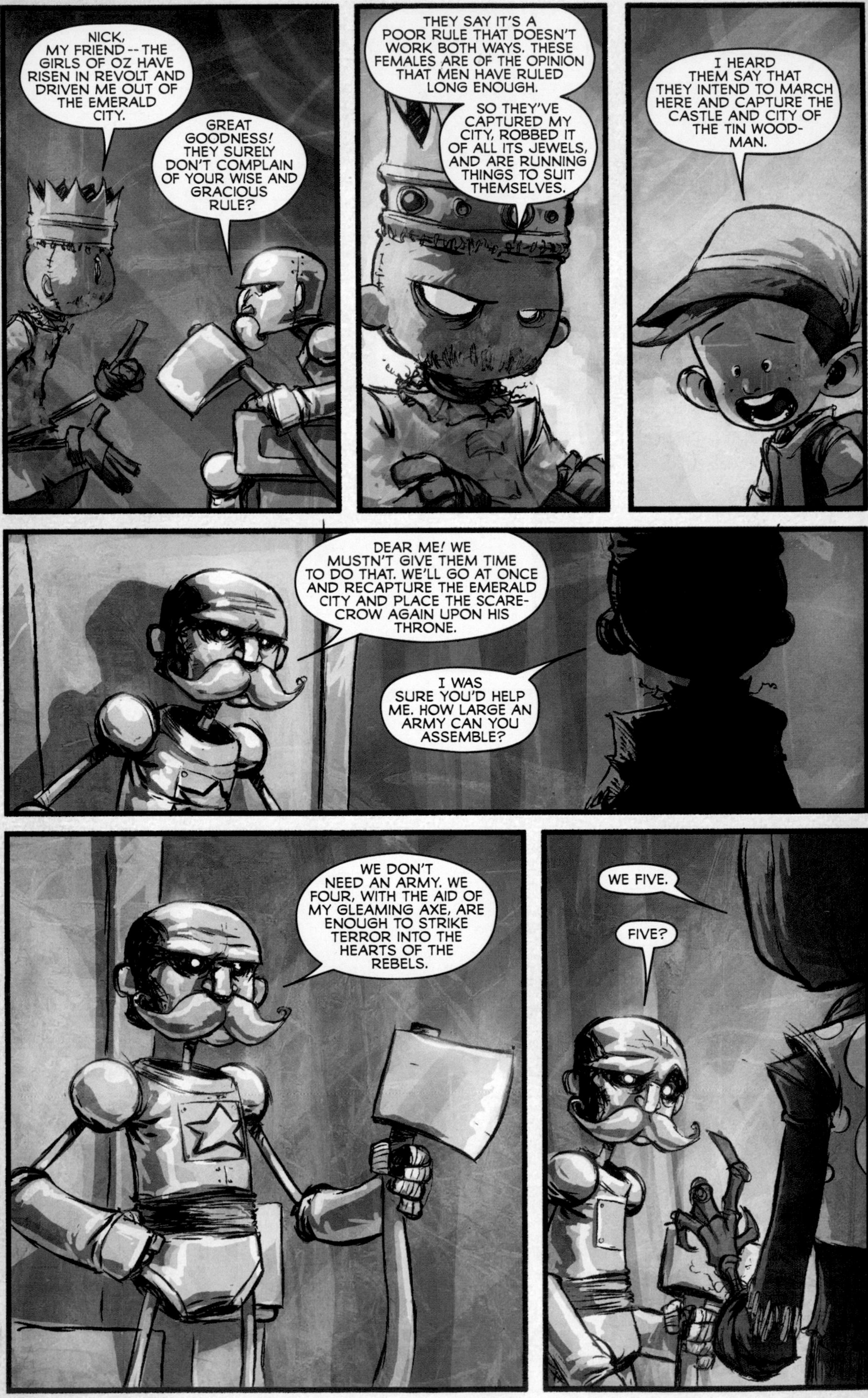
NICK, MY FRIEND -- THE GIRLS OF OZ HAVE RISEN IN REVOLT AND DRIVEN ME OUT OF THE EMERALD CITY.
GREAT GOODNESS! THEY SURELY DON'T COMPLAIN OF YOUR WISE AND GRACIOUS RULE?
THEY SAY IT'S A POOR RULE THAT DOESN'T WORK BOTH WAYS. THESE FEMALES ARE OF THE OPINION THAT MEN HAVE RULED LONG ENOUGH.
SO THEY'VE CAPTURED MY CITY, ROBBED IT OF ALL ITS JEWELS, AND ARE RUNNING THINGS TO SUIT THEMSELVES.
I HEARD THEM SAY THAT THEY INTEND TO MARCH HERE AND CAPTURE THE CASTLE AND CITY OF THE TIN WOOD-MAN.
DEAR ME! WE MUSTN'T GIVE THEM TIME TO DO THAT. WE'LL GO AT ONCE AND RECAPTURE THE EMERALD CITY AND PLACE THE SCARE-CROW AGAIN UPON HIS THRONE.
I WAS SURE YOU'D HELP ME. HOW LARGE AN ARMY CAN YOU ASSEMBLE?
WE DON'T NEED AN ARMY. WE FOUR, WITH THE AID OF MY GLEAMING AXE, ARE ENOUGH TO STRIKE TERROR INTO THE HEARTS OF THE REBELS.
WE FIVE.
FIVE?

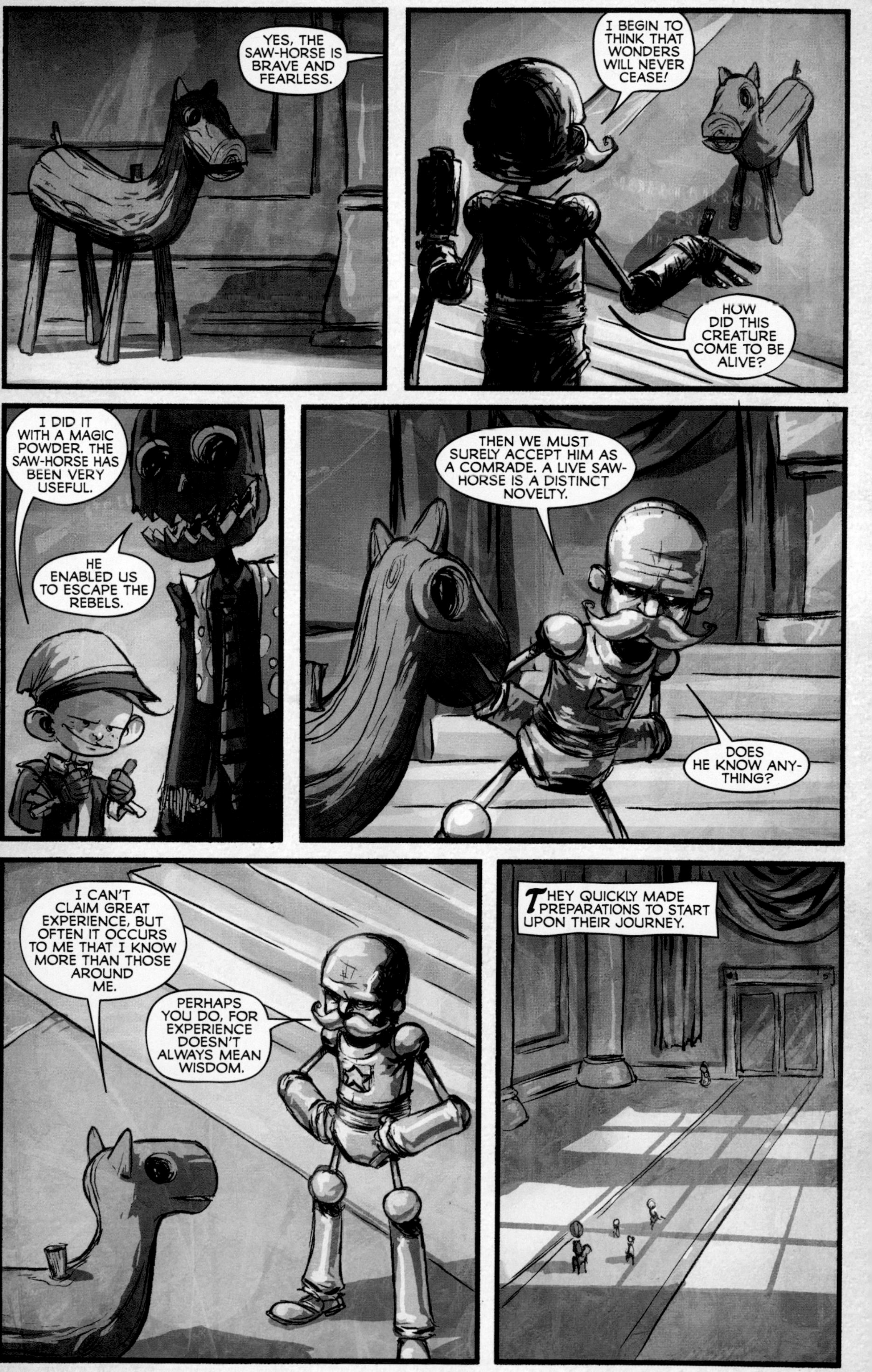

YES, THE SAW-HORSE IS BRAVE AND FEARLESS.
I BEGIN TO THINK THAT WONDERS WILL NEVER CEASE!
HOW DID THIS CREATURE COME TO BE ALIVE?
I DID IT WITH A MAGIC POWDER. THE SAW-HORSE HAS BEEN VERY USEFUL.
HE ENABLED US TO ESCAPE THE REBELS.
THEN WE MUST SURELY ACCEPT HIM AS A COMRADE. A LIVE SAW-HORSE IS A DISTINCT NOVELTY.
DOES HE KNOW ANY-THING?
I CAN'T CLAIM GREAT EXPERIENCE, BUT OFTEN IT OCCURS TO ME THAT I KNOW MORE THAN THOSE AROUND ME.
PERHAPS YOU DO, FOR EXPERIENCE DOESN'T ALWAYS MEAN WISDOM.
THEY QUICKLY MADE PREPARATIONS TO START UPON THEIR JOURNEY.

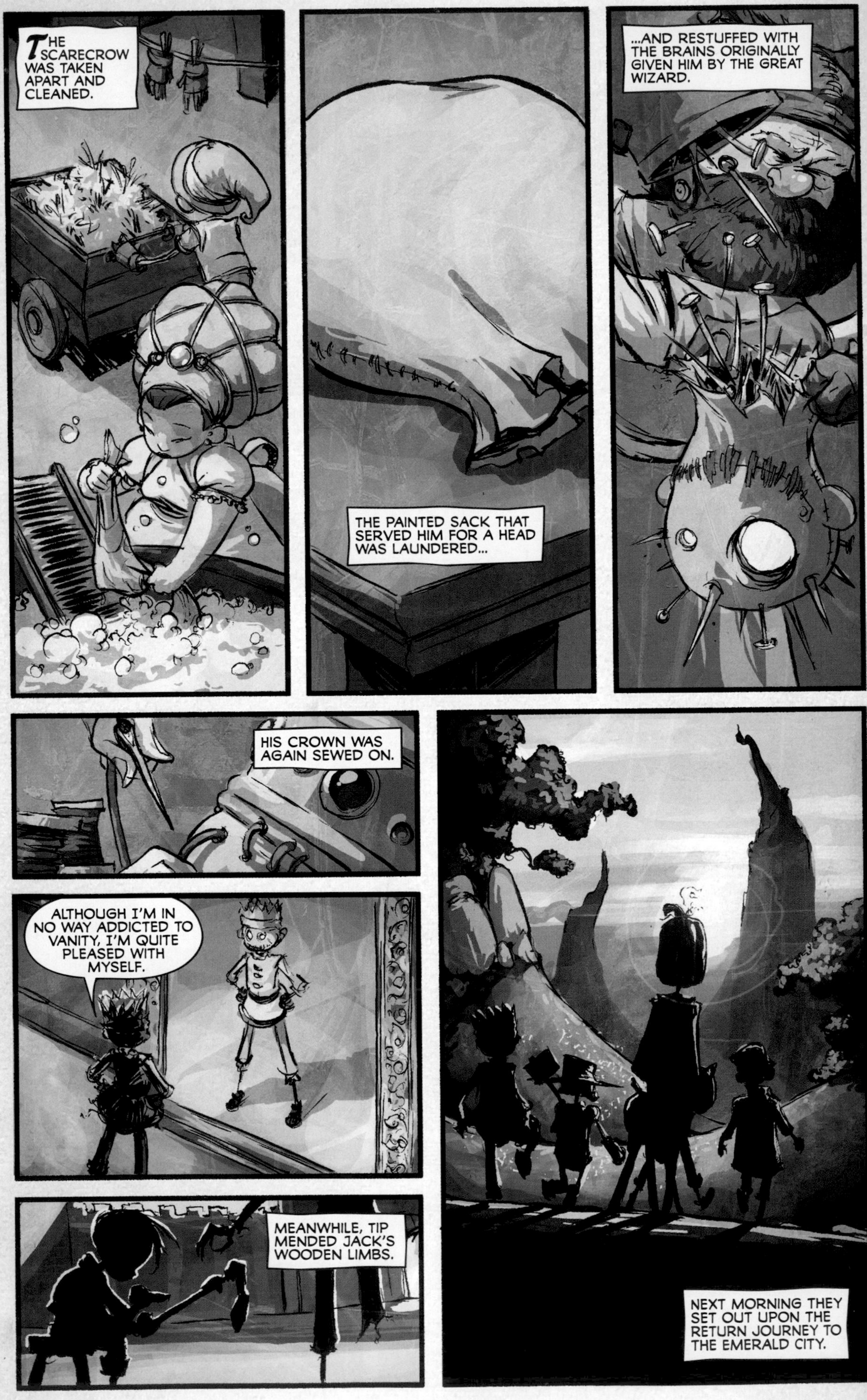
THE SCARECROW WAS TAKEN APART AND CLEANED.
THE PAINTED SACK THAT SERVED HIM FOR A HEAD WAS LAUNDERED...
...AND RESTUFFED WITH THE BRAINS ORIGINALLY GIVEN HIM BY THE GREAT WIZARD.
HIS CROWN WAS AGAIN SEWED ON.
ALTHOUGH I'M IN NO WAY ADDICTED TO VANITY, I'M QUITE PLEASED WITH MYSELF.
MEANWHILE, TIP MENDED JACK'S WOODEN LIMBS.
NEXT MORNING THEY SET OUT UPON THE RETURN JOURNEY TO THE EMERALD CITY.

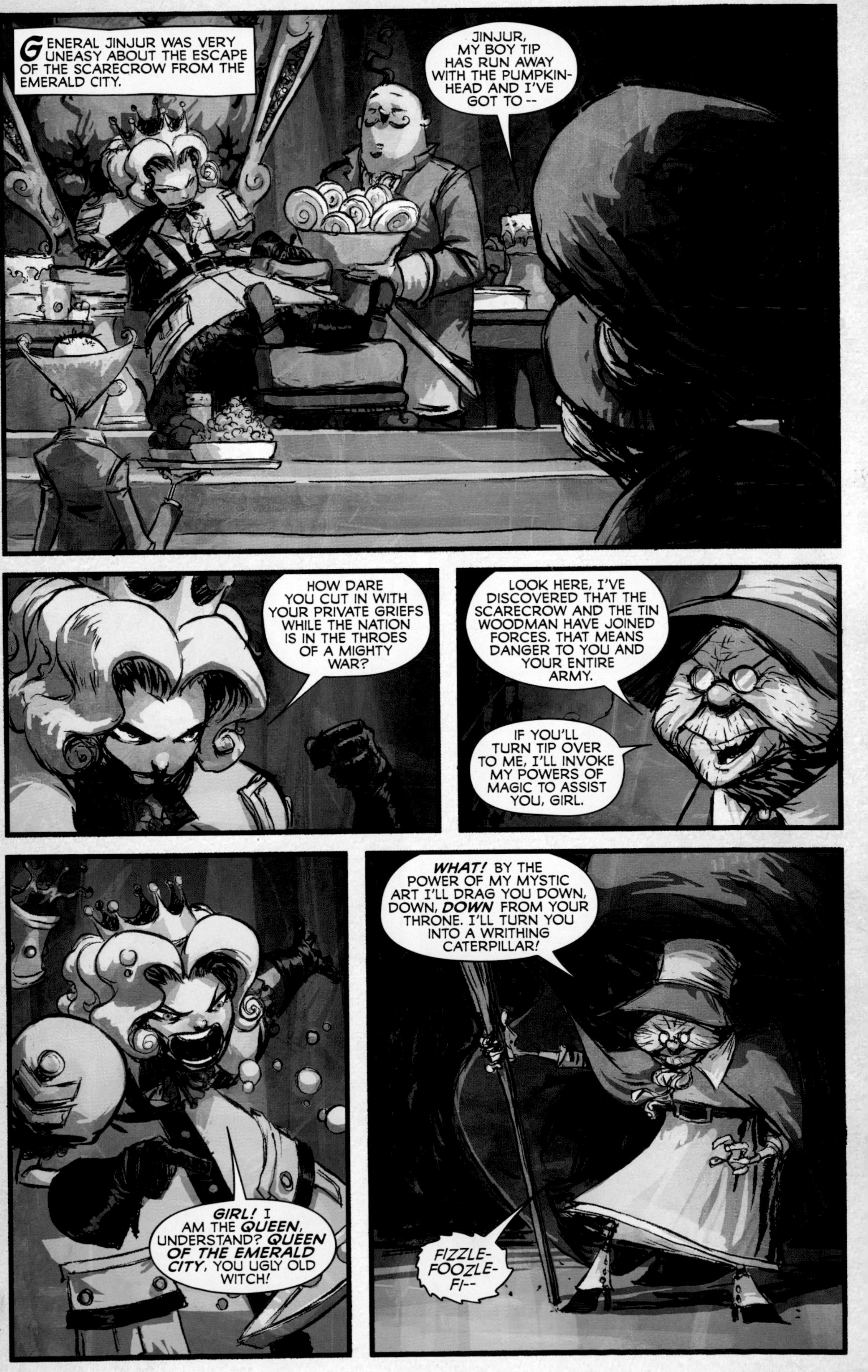
GENERAL JINJUR WAS VERY UNEASY ABOUT THE ESCAPE OF THE SCARECROW FROM THE EMERALD CITY.
JINJUR, MY BOY TIP HAS RUN AWAY WITH THE PUMPKIN-HEAD AND I'VE GOT TO --
HOW DARE YOU CUT IN WITH YOUR PRIVATE GRIEFS WHILE THE NATION IS IN THE THROES OF A MIGHTY WAR?
LOOK HERE, I'VE DISCOVERED THAT THE SCARECROW AND THE TIN WOODMAN HAVE JOINED FORCES. THAT MEANS DANGER TO YOU AND YOUR ENTIRE ARMY.
IF YOU'LL TURN TIP OVER TO ME, I'LL INVOKE MY POWERS OF MAGIC TO ASSIST YOU, GIRL.
GIRL! I AM THE QUEEN, UNDERSTAND? QUEEN OF THE EMERALD CITY, YOU UGLY OLD WITCH!
WHAT! BY THE POWER OF MY MYSTIC ART I'LL DRAG YOU DOWN, DOWN, DOWN FROM YOUR THRONE. I'LL TURN YOU INTO A WRITHING CATERPILLAR!
FIZZLE-FOOZLE-FI--

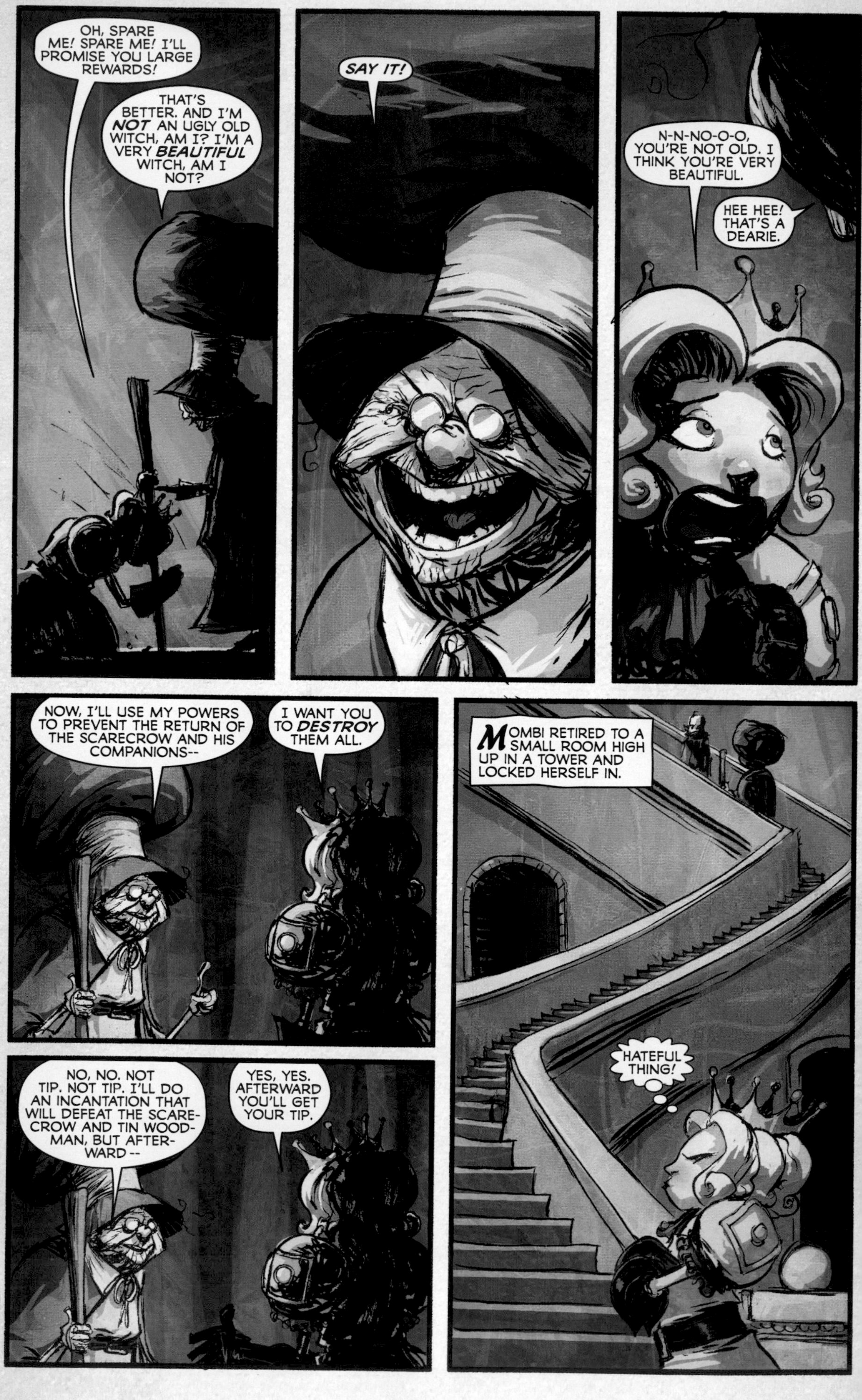
OH, SPARE ME! SPARE ME! I'LL PROMISE YOU LARGE REWARDS!
THAT'S BETTER. AND I'M **NOT** AN UGLY OLD WITCH, AM I? I'M A VERY **BEAUTIFUL** WITCH, AM I NOT?
SAY IT!
N-N-NO-O-O, YOU'RE NOT OLD. I THINK YOU'RE VERY BEAUTIFUL.
HEE HEE! THAT'S A DEARIE.
NOW, I'LL USE MY POWERS TO PREVENT THE RETURN OF THE SCARECROW AND HIS COMPANIONS--
I WANT YOU TO **DESTROY** THEM ALL.
NO, NO. NOT TIP. NOT TIP. I'LL DO AN INCANTATION THAT WILL DEFEAT THE SCARE-CROW AND TIN WOOD-MAN, BUT AFTER-WARD --
YES, YES. AFTERWARD YOU'LL GET YOUR TIP.
MOMBI RETIRED TO A SMALL ROOM HIGH UP IN A TOWER AND LOCKED HERSELF IN.
HATEFUL THING!

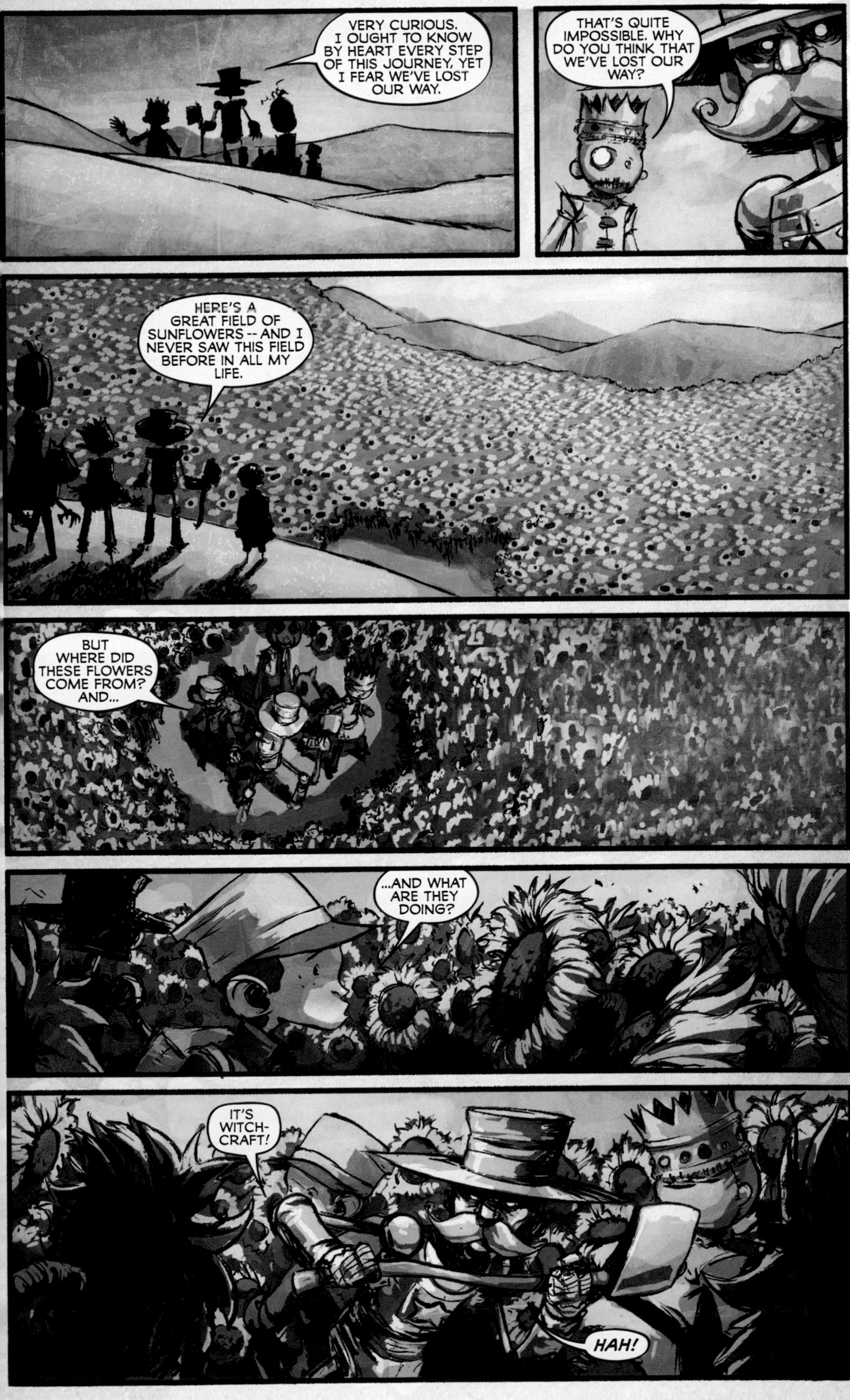
VERY CURIOUS. I OUGHT TO KNOW BY HEART EVERY STEP OF THIS JOURNEY, YET I FEAR WE'VE LOST OUR WAY.
THAT'S QUITE IMPOSSIBLE. WHY DO YOU THINK THAT WE'VE LOST OUR WAY?
HERE'S A GREAT FIELD OF SUNFLOWERS -- AND I NEVER SAW THIS FIELD BEFORE IN ALL MY LIFE.
BUT WHERE DID THESE FLOWERS COME FROM? AND...
...AND WHAT ARE THEY DOING?
IT'S WITCH-CRAFT!
HAH!

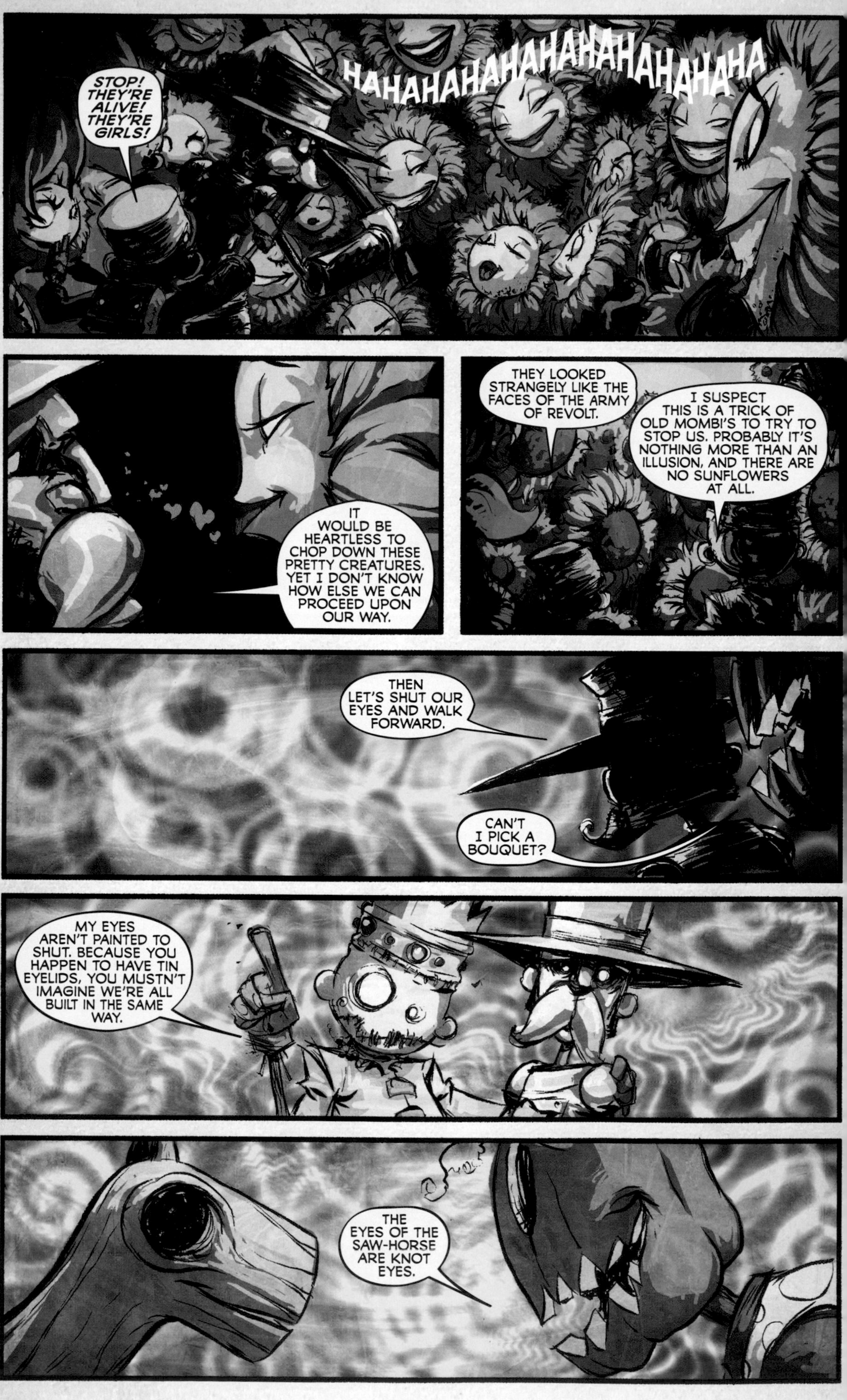
STOP! THEY'RE ALIVE! THEY'RE GIRLS!
HAHAHAHAHAHAHAHAHAHAHA
IT WOULD BE HEARTLESS TO CHOP DOWN THESE PRETTY CREATURES. YET I DON'T KNOW HOW ELSE WE CAN PROCEED UPON OUR WAY.
THEY LOOKED STRANGELY LIKE THE FACES OF THE ARMY OF REVOLT.
I SUSPECT THIS IS A TRICK OF OLD MOMBI'S TO TRY TO STOP US. PROBABLY IT'S NOTHING MORE THAN AN ILLUSION, AND THERE ARE NO SUNFLOWERS AT ALL.
THEN LET'S SHUT OUR EYES AND WALK FORWARD.
CAN'T I PICK A BOUQUET?
MY EYES AREN'T PAINTED TO SHUT. BECAUSE YOU HAPPEN TO HAVE TIN EYELIDS, YOU MUSTN'T IMAGINE WE'RE ALL BUILT IN THE SAME WAY.
THE EYES OF THE SAW-HORSE ARE KNOT EYES.

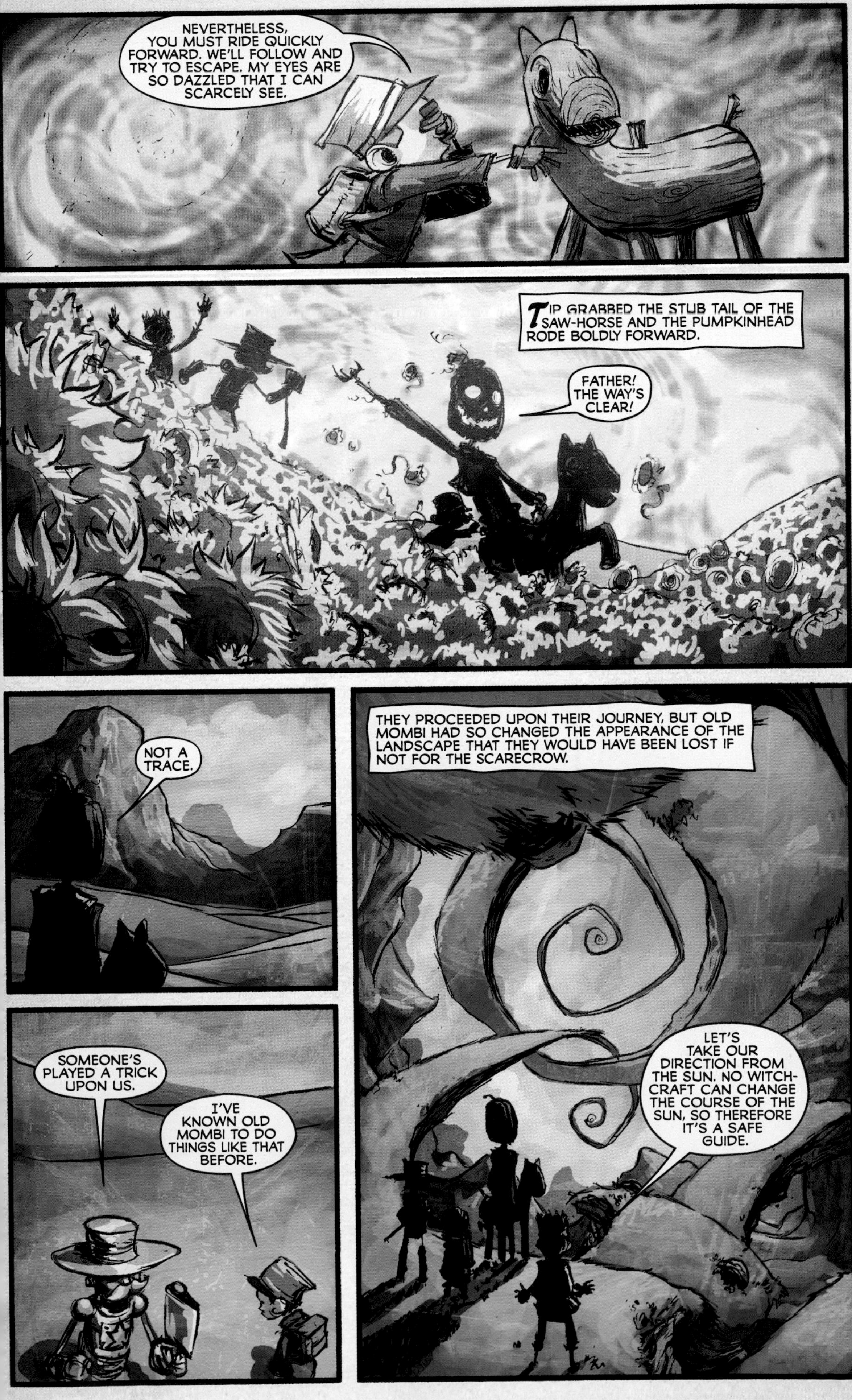
NEVERTHELESS, YOU MUST RIDE QUICKLY FORWARD. WE'LL FOLLOW AND TRY TO ESCAPE. MY EYES ARE SO DAZZLED THAT I CAN SCARCELY SEE.
TIP GRABBED THE STUB TAIL OF THE SAW-HORSE AND THE PUMPKINHEAD RODE BOLDLY FORWARD.
FATHER! THE WAY'S CLEAR!
NOT A TRACE.
SOMEONE'S PLAYED A TRICK UPON US.
I'VE KNOWN OLD MOMBI TO DO THINGS LIKE THAT BEFORE.
THEY PROCEEDED UPON THEIR JOURNEY, BUT OLD MOMBI HAD SO CHANGED THE APPEARANCE OF THE LANDSCAPE THAT THEY WOULD HAVE BEEN LOST IF NOT FOR THE SCARECROW.
LET'S TAKE OUR DIRECTION FROM THE SUN. NO WITCH-CRAFT CAN CHANGE THE COURSE OF THE SUN, SO THEREFORE IT'S A SAFE GUIDE.

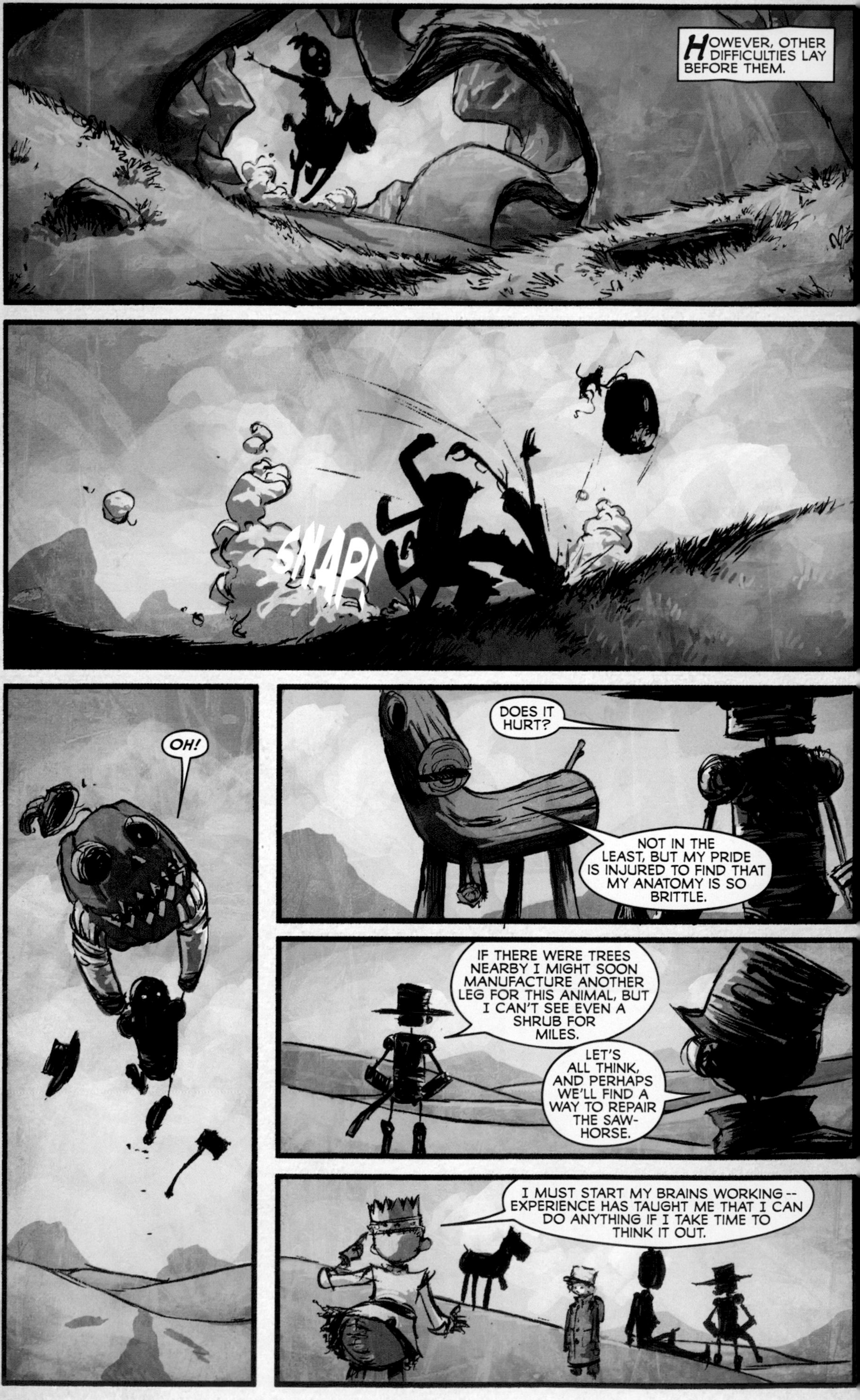
HOWEVER, OTHER DIFFICULTIES LAY BEFORE THEM.
SNAP!
OH!
DOES IT HURT?
NOT IN THE LEAST, BUT MY PRIDE IS INJURED TO FIND THAT MY ANATOMY IS SO BRITTLE.
IF THERE WERE TREES NEARBY I MIGHT SOON MANUFACTURE ANOTHER LEG FOR THIS ANIMAL, BUT I CAN'T SEE EVEN A SHRUB FOR MILES.
LET'S ALL THINK, AND PERHAPS WE'LL FIND A WAY TO REPAIR THE SAW-HORSE.
I MUST START MY BRAINS WORKING -- EXPERIENCE HAS TAUGHT ME THAT I CAN DO ANYTHING IF I TAKE TIME TO THINK IT OUT.

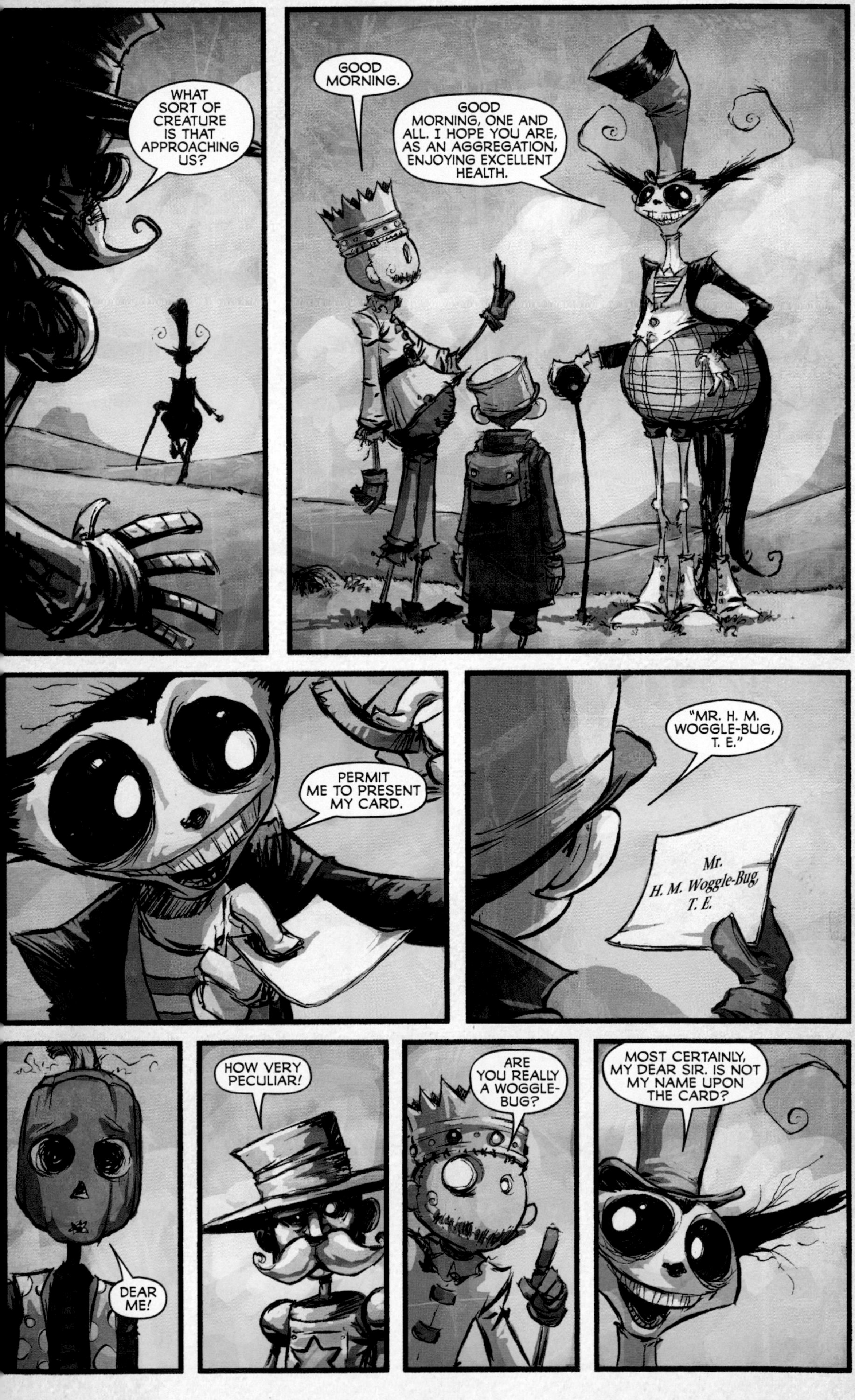
WHAT SORT OF CREATURE IS THAT APPROACHING US?
GOOD MORNING.
GOOD MORNING, ONE AND ALL. I HOPE YOU ARE, AS AN AGGREGATION, ENJOYING EXCELLENT HEALTH.
PERMIT ME TO PRESENT MY CARD.
"MR. H. M. WOGGLE-BUG, T. E."
Mr. H. M. Woggle-Bug, T. E.
DEAR ME!
HOW VERY PECULIAR!
ARE YOU REALLY A WOGGLE-BUG?
MOST CERTAINLY, MY DEAR SIR. IS NOT MY NAME UPON THE CARD?

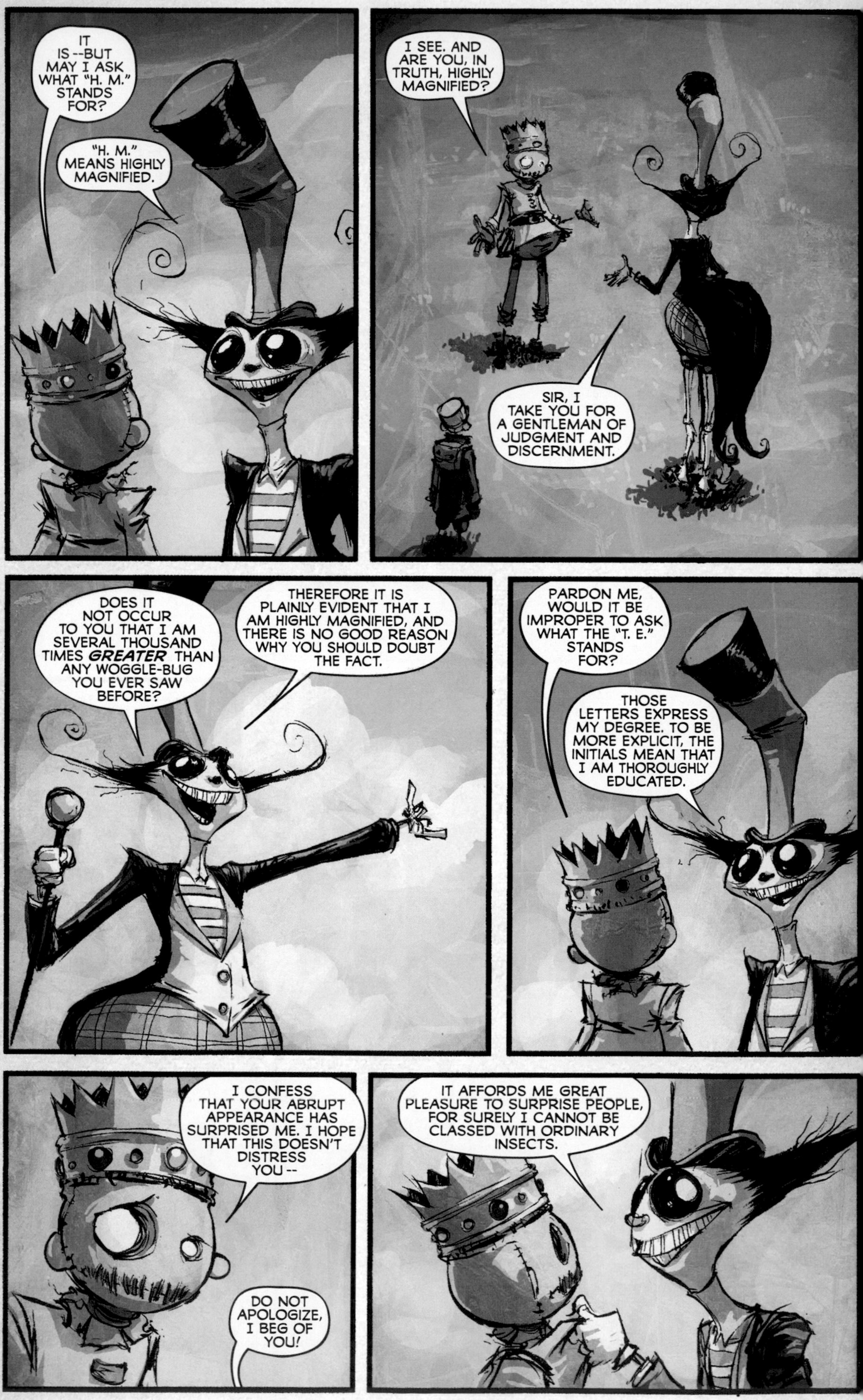
IT IS --BUT MAY I ASK WHAT "H. M." STANDS FOR?
"H. M." MEANS HIGHLY MAGNIFIED.
I SEE. AND ARE YOU, IN TRUTH, HIGHLY MAGNIFIED?
SIR, I TAKE YOU FOR A GENTLEMAN OF JUDGMENT AND DISCERNMENT.
DOES IT NOT OCCUR TO YOU THAT I AM SEVERAL THOUSAND TIMES GREATER THAN ANY WOGGLE-BUG YOU EVER SAW BEFORE?
THEREFORE IT IS PLAINLY EVIDENT THAT I AM HIGHLY MAGNIFIED, AND THERE IS NO GOOD REASON WHY YOU SHOULD DOUBT THE FACT.
PARDON ME, WOULD IT BE IMPROPER TO ASK WHAT THE "T. E." STANDS FOR?
THOSE LETTERS EXPRESS MY DEGREE. TO BE MORE EXPLICIT, THE INITIALS MEAN THAT I AM THOROUGHLY EDUCATED.
I CONFESS THAT YOUR ABRUPT APPEARANCE HAS SURPRISED ME. I HOPE THAT THIS DOESN'T DISTRESS YOU --
DO NOT APOLOGIZE, I BEG OF YOU!
IT AFFORDS ME GREAT PLEASURE TO SURPRISE PEOPLE, FOR SURELY I CANNOT BE CLASSED WITH ORDINARY INSECTS.

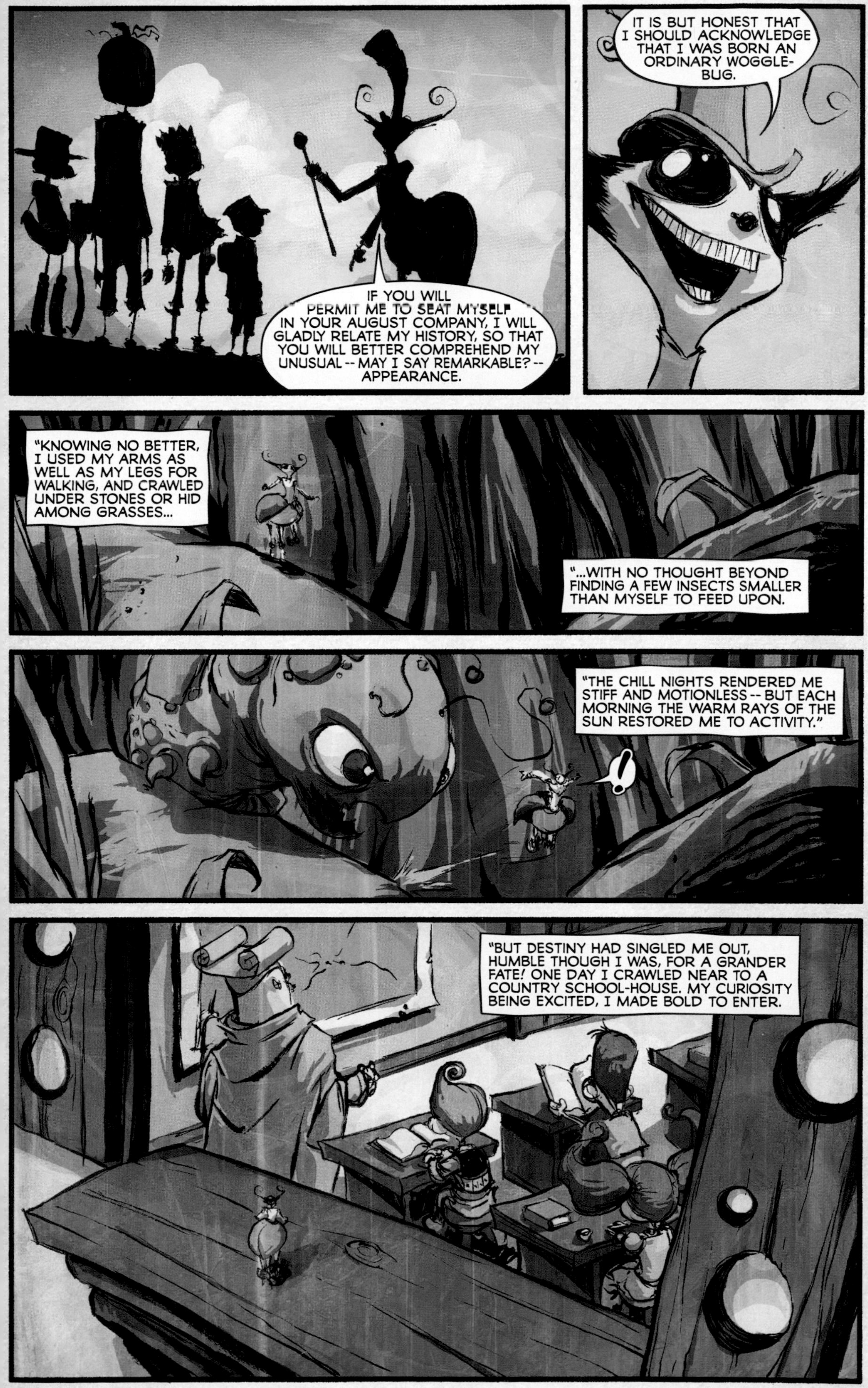
IF YOU WILL PERMIT ME TO SEAT MYSELF IN YOUR AUGUST COMPANY, I WILL GLADLY RELATE MY HISTORY, SO THAT YOU WILL BETTER COMPREHEND MY UNUSUAL -- MAY I SAY REMARKABLE? -- APPEARANCE.
IT IS BUT HONEST THAT I SHOULD ACKNOWLEDGE THAT I WAS BORN AN ORDINARY WOGGLE-BUG.
"KNOWING NO BETTER, I USED MY ARMS AS WELL AS MY LEGS FOR WALKING, AND CRAWLED UNDER STONES OR HID AMONG GRASSES...
"...WITH NO THOUGHT BEYOND FINDING A FEW INSECTS SMALLER THAN MYSELF TO FEED UPON.
"THE CHILL NIGHTS RENDERED ME STIFF AND MOTIONLESS -- BUT EACH MORNING THE WARM RAYS OF THE SUN RESTORED ME TO ACTIVITY."
!
"BUT DESTINY HAD SINGLED ME OUT, HUMBLE THOUGH I WAS, FOR A GRANDER FATE! ONE DAY I CRAWLED NEAR TO A COUNTRY SCHOOL-HOUSE. MY CURIOSITY BEING EXCITED, I MADE BOLD TO ENTER.

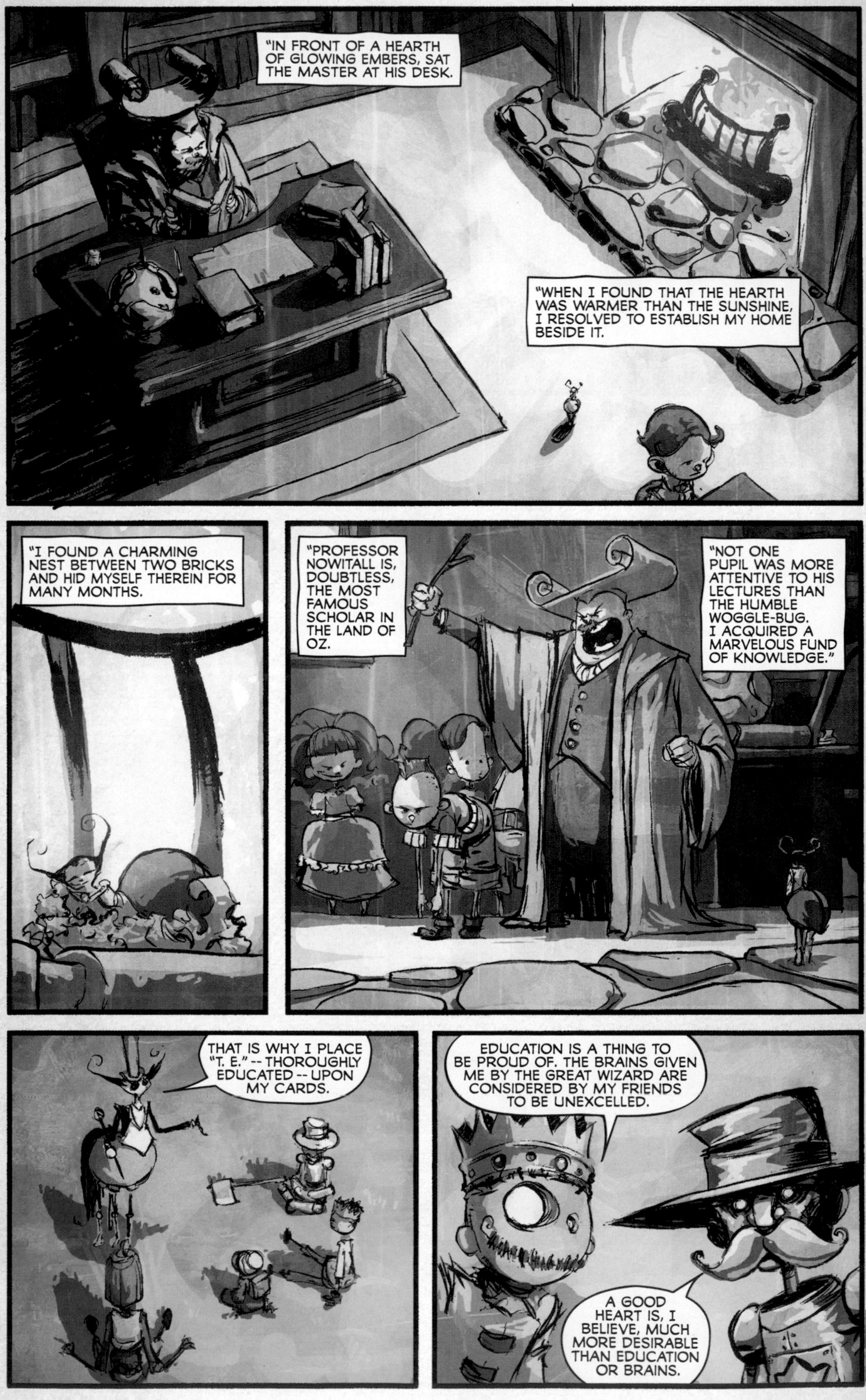
"IN FRONT OF A HEARTH OF GLOWING EMBERS, SAT THE MASTER AT HIS DESK.
"WHEN I FOUND THAT THE HEARTH WAS WARMER THAN THE SUNSHINE, I RESOLVED TO ESTABLISH MY HOME BESIDE IT.
"I FOUND A CHARMING NEST BETWEEN TWO BRICKS AND HID MYSELF THEREIN FOR MANY MONTHS.
"PROFESSOR NOWITALL IS, DOUBTLESS, THE MOST FAMOUS SCHOLAR IN THE LAND OF OZ.
"NOT ONE PUPIL WAS MORE ATTENTIVE TO HIS LECTURES THAN THE HUMBLE WOGGLE-BUG. I ACQUIRED A MARVELOUS FUND OF KNOWLEDGE."
THAT IS WHY I PLACE "T. E." -- THOROUGHLY EDUCATED -- UPON MY CARDS.
EDUCATION IS A THING TO BE PROUD OF. THE BRAINS GIVEN ME BY THE GREAT WIZARD ARE CONSIDERED BY MY FRIENDS TO BE UNEXCELLED.
A GOOD HEART IS, I BELIEVE, MUCH MORE DESIRABLE THAN EDUCATION OR BRAINS.

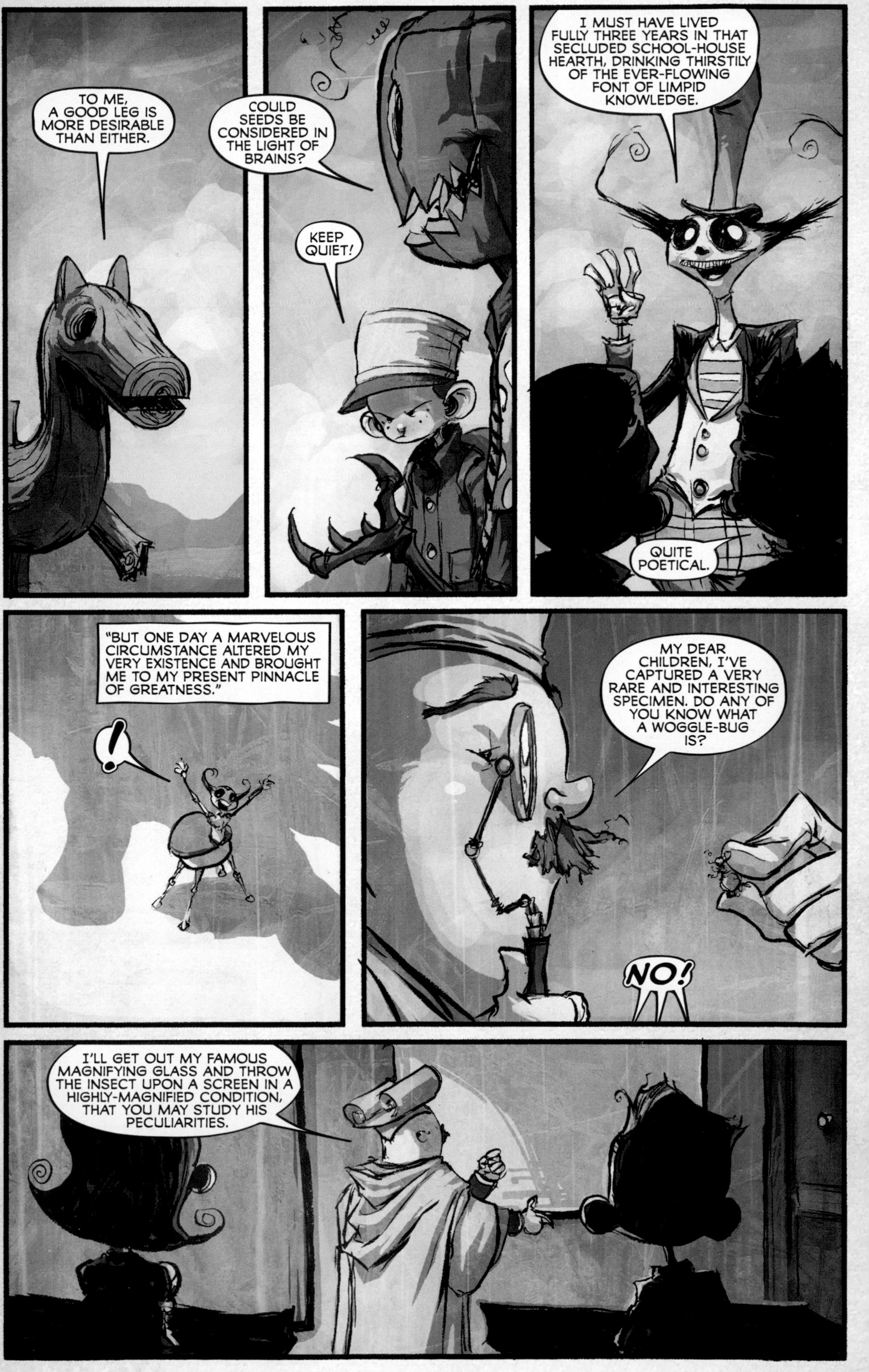
TO ME, A GOOD LEG IS MORE DESIRABLE THAN EITHER.
COULD SEEDS BE CONSIDERED IN THE LIGHT OF BRAINS?
KEEP QUIET!
I MUST HAVE LIVED FULLY THREE YEARS IN THAT SECLUDED SCHOOL-HOUSE HEARTH, DRINKING THIRSTILY OF THE EVER-FLOWING FONT OF LIMPID KNOWLEDGE.
QUITE POETICAL.
"BUT ONE DAY A MARVELOUS CIRCUMSTANCE ALTERED MY VERY EXISTENCE AND BROUGHT ME TO MY PRESENT PINNACLE OF GREATNESS."
!
MY DEAR CHILDREN, I'VE CAPTURED A VERY RARE AND INTERESTING SPECIMEN. DO ANY OF YOU KNOW WHAT A WOGGLE-BUG IS?
NO!
I'LL GET OUT MY FAMOUS MAGNIFYING GLASS AND THROW THE INSECT UPON A SCREEN IN A HIGHLY-MAGNIFIED CONDITION, THAT YOU MAY STUDY HIS PECULIARITIES.

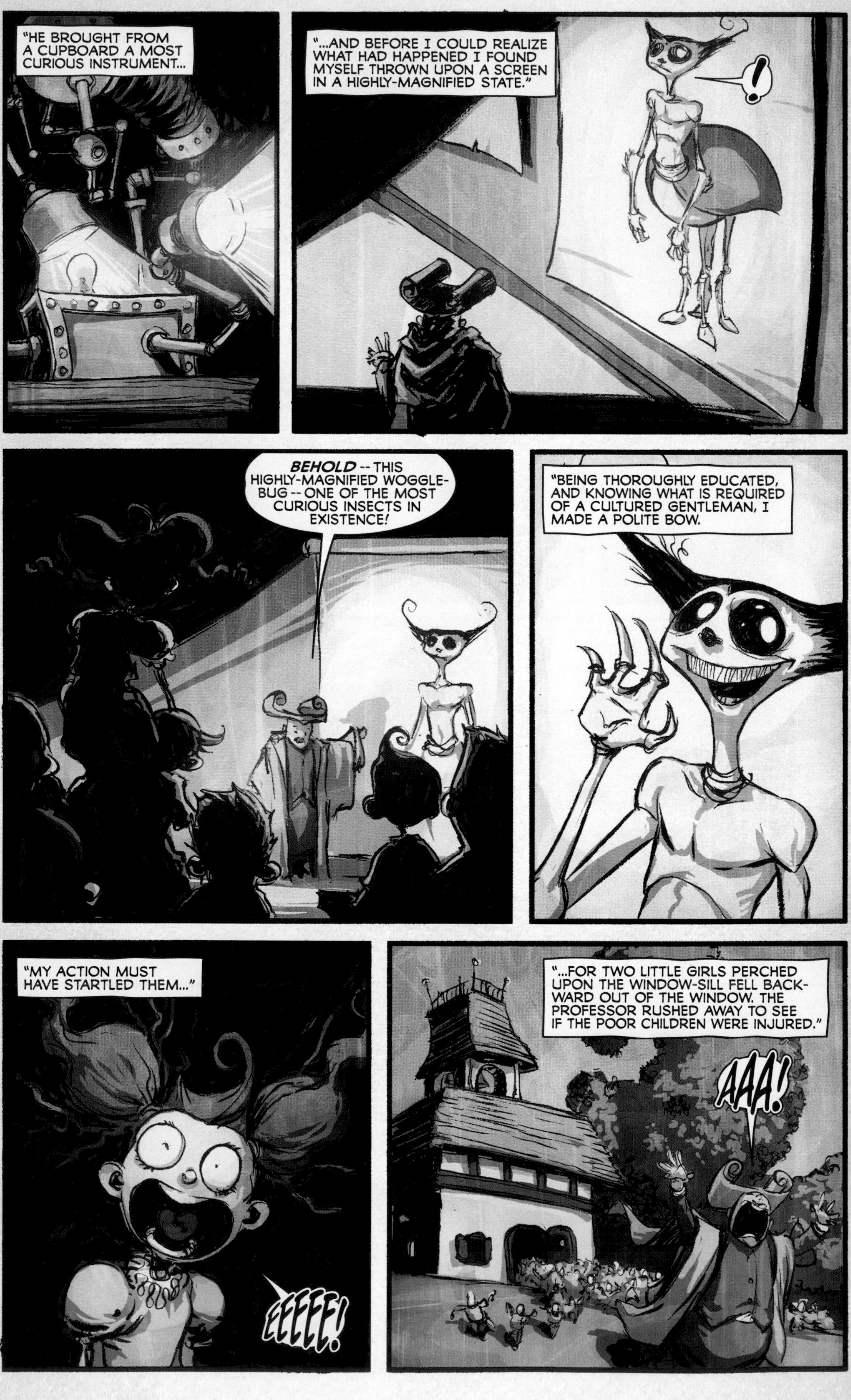
"HE BROUGHT FROM A CUPBOARD A MOST CURIOUS INSTRUMENT...
"...AND BEFORE I COULD REALIZE WHAT HAD HAPPENED I FOUND MYSELF THROWN UPON A SCREEN IN A HIGHLY-MAGNIFIED STATE."
!
BEHOLD -- THIS HIGHLY-MAGNIFIED WOGGLE-BUG -- ONE OF THE MOST CURIOUS INSECTS IN EXISTENCE!
"BEING THOROUGHLY EDUCATED, AND KNOWING WHAT IS REQUIRED OF A CULTURED GENTLEMAN, I MADE A POLITE BOW.
"MY ACTION MUST HAVE STARTLED THEM..."
EEEEE!
"...FOR TWO LITTLE GIRLS PERCHED UPON THE WINDOW-SILL FELL BACKWARD OUT OF THE WINDOW. THE PROFESSOR RUSHED AWAY TO SEE IF THE POOR CHILDREN WERE INJURED."
AAA!

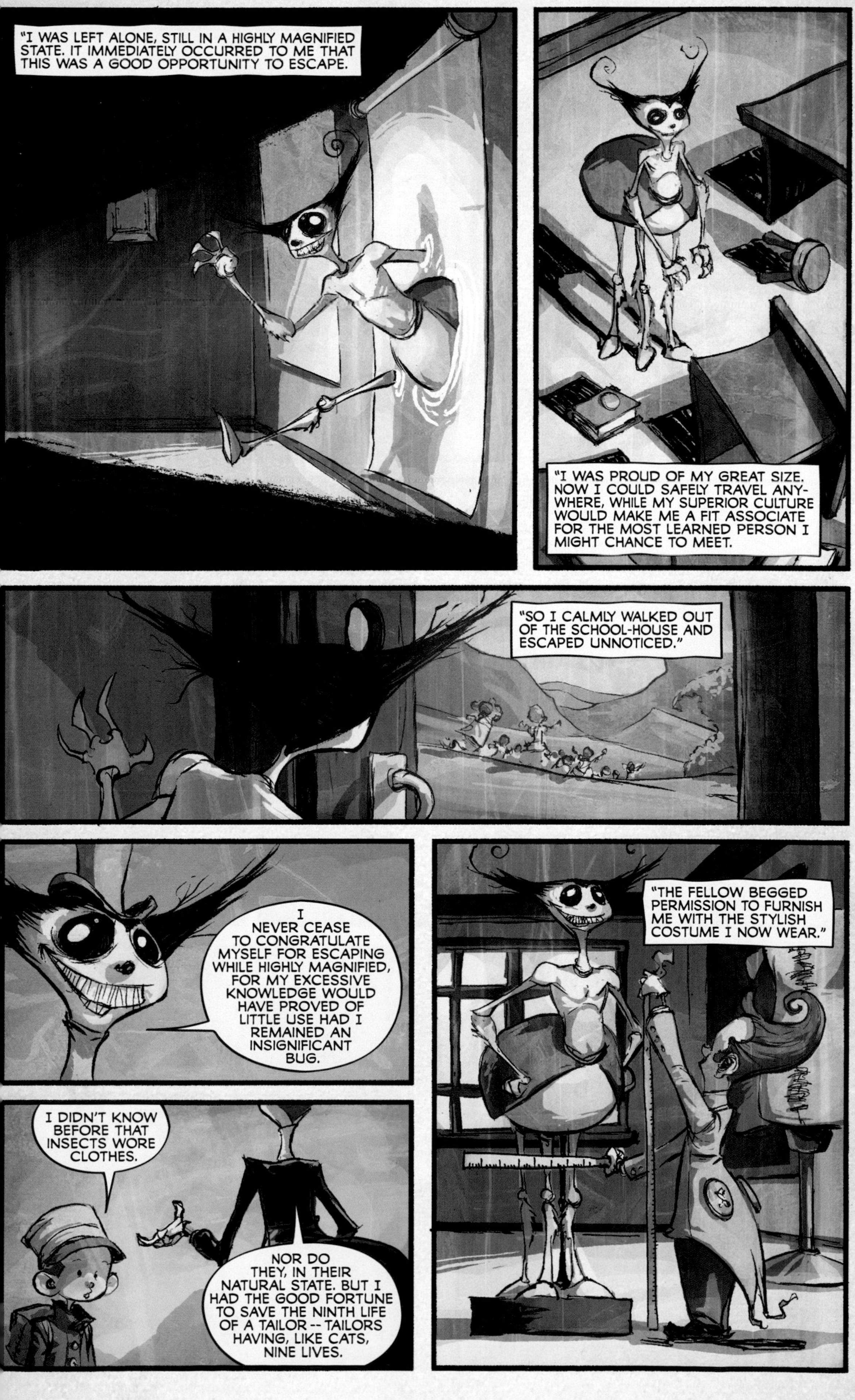
"I WAS LEFT ALONE, STILL IN A HIGHLY MAGNIFIED STATE. IT IMMEDIATELY OCCURRED TO ME THAT THIS WAS A GOOD OPPORTUNITY TO ESCAPE.
"I WAS PROUD OF MY GREAT SIZE. NOW I COULD SAFELY TRAVEL ANY-WHERE, WHILE MY SUPERIOR CULTURE WOULD MAKE ME A FIT ASSOCIATE FOR THE MOST LEARNED PERSON I MIGHT CHANCE TO MEET.
"SO I CALMLY WALKED OUT OF THE SCHOOL-HOUSE AND ESCAPED UNNOTICED."
I NEVER CEASE TO CONGRATULATE MYSELF FOR ESCAPING WHILE HIGHLY MAGNIFIED, FOR MY EXCESSIVE KNOWLEDGE WOULD HAVE PROVED OF LITTLE USE HAD I REMAINED AN INSIGNIFICANT BUG.
I DIDN'T KNOW BEFORE THAT INSECTS WORE CLOTHES.
NOR DO THEY, IN THEIR NATURAL STATE. BUT I HAD THE GOOD FORTUNE TO SAVE THE NINTH LIFE OF A TAILOR -- TAILORS HAVING, LIKE CATS, NINE LIVES.
"THE FELLOW BEGGED PERMISSION TO FURNISH ME WITH THE STYLISH COSTUME I NOW WEAR."

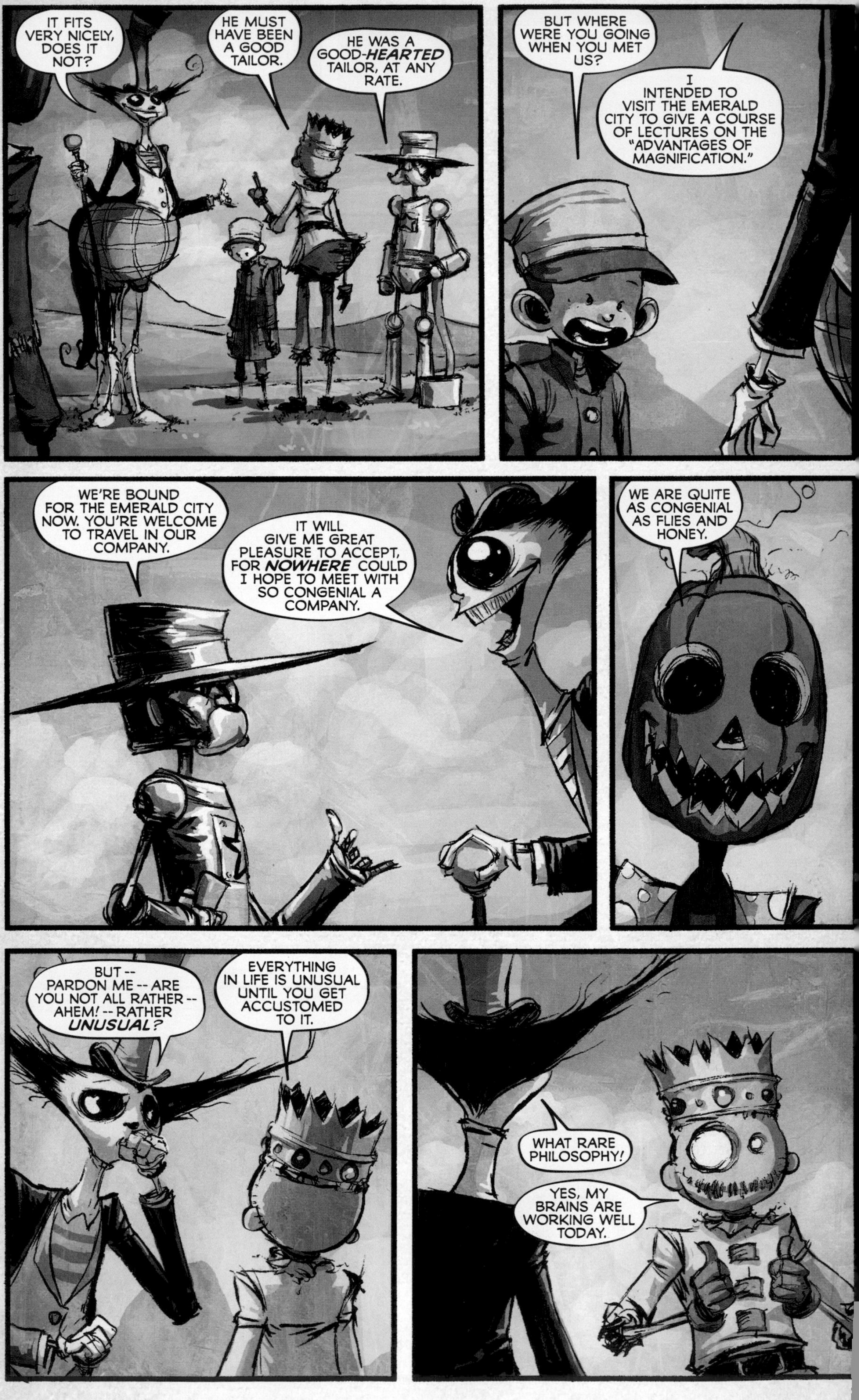
IT FITS VERY NICELY, DOES IT NOT?
HE MUST HAVE BEEN A GOOD TAILOR.
HE WAS A GOOD-*HEARTED* TAILOR, AT ANY RATE.
BUT WHERE WERE YOU GOING WHEN YOU MET US?
I INTENDED TO VISIT THE EMERALD CITY TO GIVE A COURSE OF LECTURES ON THE "ADVANTAGES OF MAGNIFICATION."
WE'RE BOUND FOR THE EMERALD CITY NOW. YOU'RE WELCOME TO TRAVEL IN OUR COMPANY.
IT WILL GIVE ME GREAT PLEASURE TO ACCEPT, FOR *NOWHERE* COULD I HOPE TO MEET WITH SO CONGENIAL A COMPANY.
WE ARE QUITE AS CONGENIAL AS FLIES AND HONEY.
BUT -- PARDON ME -- ARE YOU NOT ALL RATHER -- AHEM! -- RATHER *UNUSUAL?*
EVERYTHING IN LIFE IS UNUSUAL UNTIL YOU GET ACCUSTOMED TO IT.
WHAT RARE PHILOSOPHY!
YES, MY BRAINS ARE WORKING WELL TODAY.

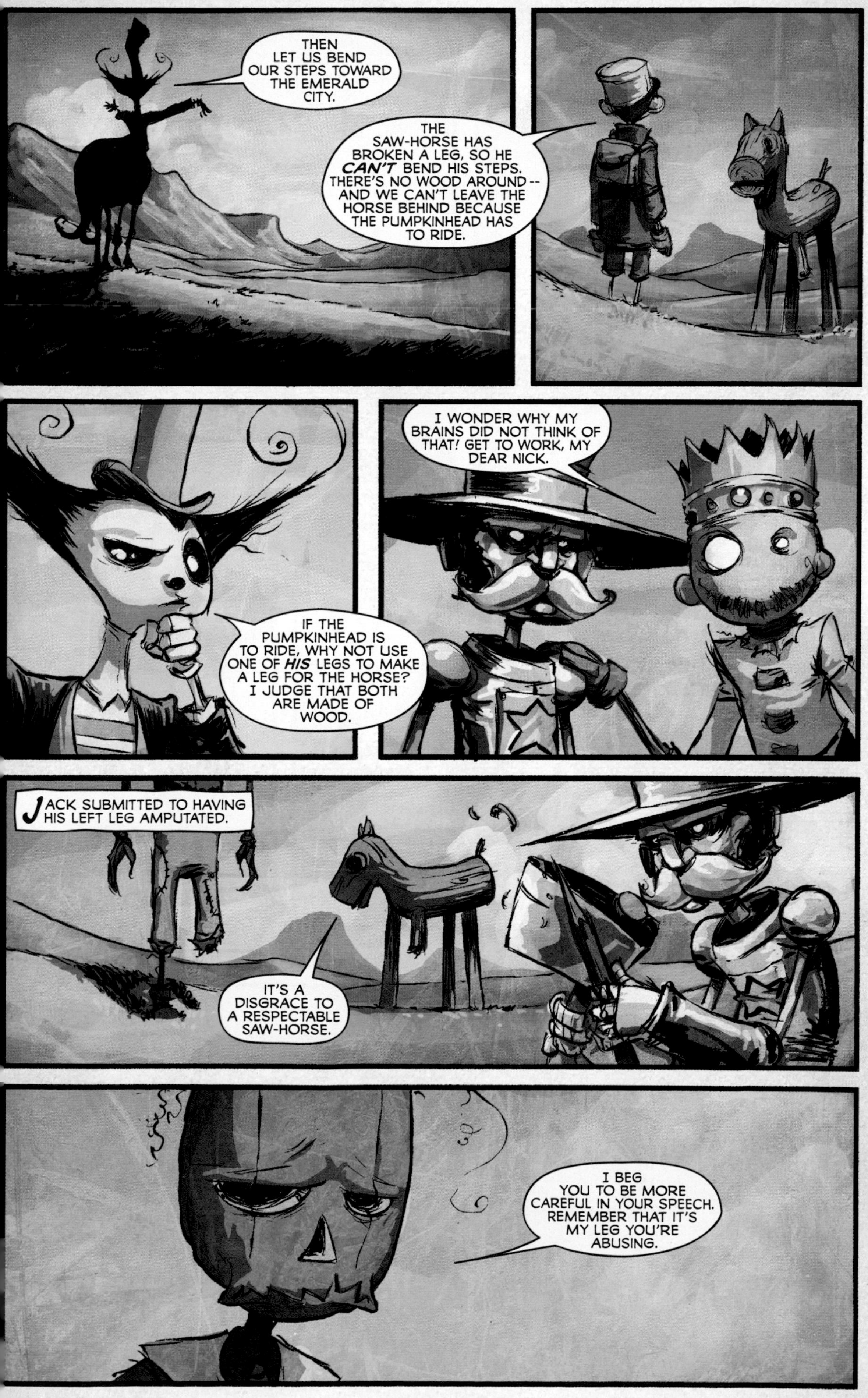
THEN LET US BEND OUR STEPS TOWARD THE EMERALD CITY.
THE SAW-HORSE HAS BROKEN A LEG, SO HE CAN'T BEND HIS STEPS. THERE'S NO WOOD AROUND -- AND WE CAN'T LEAVE THE HORSE BEHIND BECAUSE THE PUMPKINHEAD HAS TO RIDE.
IF THE PUMPKINHEAD IS TO RIDE, WHY NOT USE ONE OF HIS LEGS TO MAKE A LEG FOR THE HORSE? I JUDGE THAT BOTH ARE MADE OF WOOD.
I WONDER WHY MY BRAINS DID NOT THINK OF THAT! GET TO WORK, MY DEAR NICK.
JACK SUBMITTED TO HAVING HIS LEFT LEG AMPUTATED.
IT'S A DISGRACE TO A RESPECTABLE SAW-HORSE.
I BEG YOU TO BE MORE CAREFUL IN YOUR SPEECH. REMEMBER THAT IT'S MY LEG YOU'RE ABUSING.

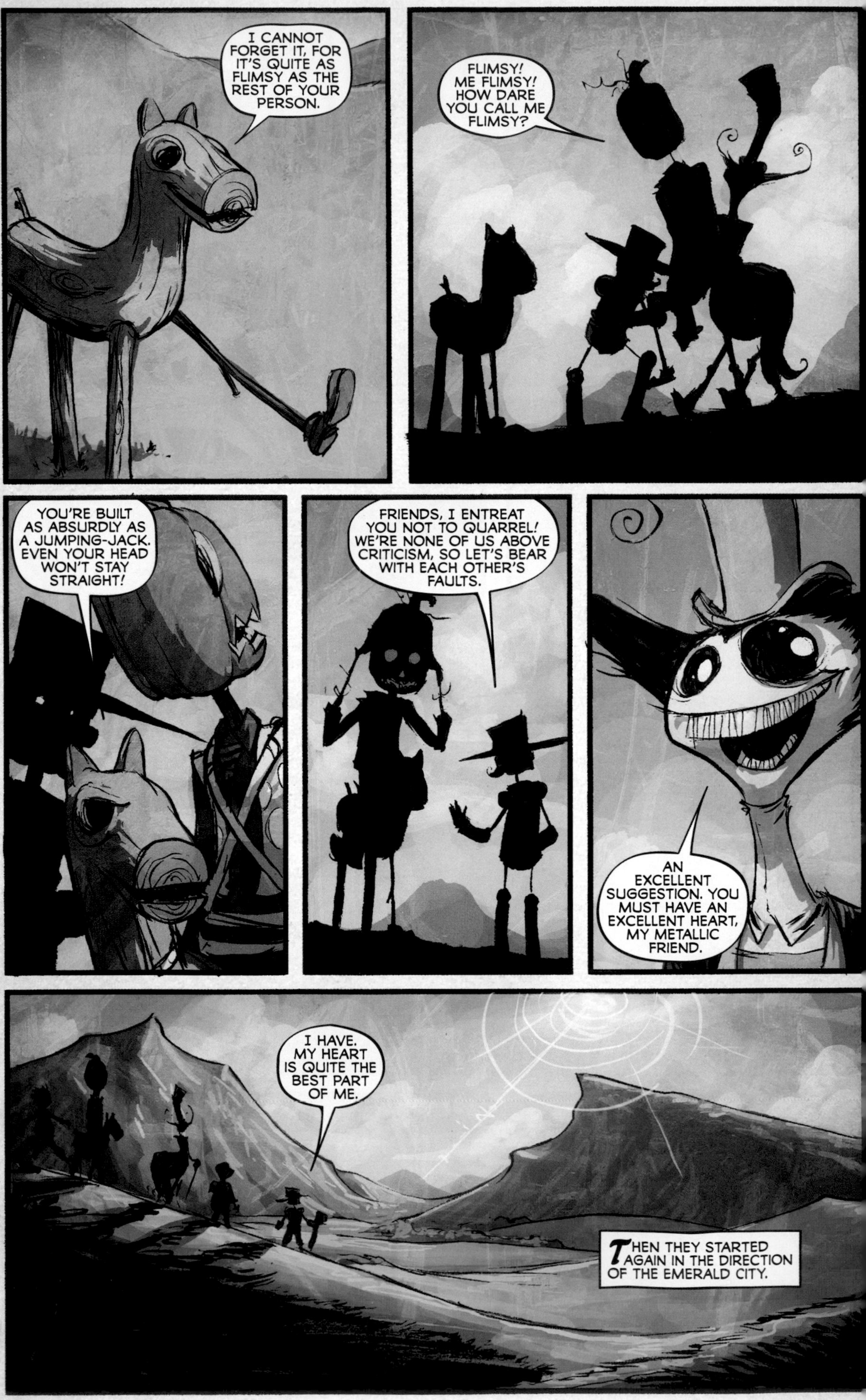
I CANNOT FORGET IT, FOR IT'S QUITE AS FLIMSY AS THE REST OF YOUR PERSON.
FLIMSY! ME FLIMSY! HOW DARE YOU CALL ME FLIMSY?
YOU'RE BUILT AS ABSURDLY AS A JUMPING-JACK. EVEN YOUR HEAD WON'T STAY STRAIGHT!
FRIENDS, I ENTREAT YOU NOT TO QUARREL! WE'RE NONE OF US ABOVE CRITICISM, SO LET'S BEAR WITH EACH OTHER'S FAULTS.
AN EXCELLENT SUGGESTION. YOU MUST HAVE AN EXCELLENT HEART, MY METALLIC FRIEND.
I HAVE. MY HEART IS QUITE THE BEST PART OF ME.
THEN THEY STARTED AGAIN IN THE DIRECTION OF THE EMERALD CITY.